Alan and the Animals

by Evelyn Foster

Illustrated by Richard Morgan

W
FRANKLIN WATTS

Notes on the series

TIDDLERS are structured to provide support for newly independent readers. The stories may also be used by adults for sharing with young children.

Starting to read alone can be daunting. **TIDDLERS** help by listing the words in the book for a check before reading, and by providing visual support and repeating words and phrases. These books will both develop confidence and encourage reading and rereading for pleasure.

If you are reading this book with a child, here are a few suggestions:

1. Make reading fun! Choose a time to read when you and the child are relaxed and have time to share the story.
2. Talk about the story before you start reading. Look at the cover and the blurb. What might the story be about? Why might the child like it?
3. Look also at the list of words below - can the child tackle most of the words?
4. Encourage the child to retell the story, using the jumbled picture puzzle.
5. Give praise! Remember that small mistakes need not always be corrected.

Here is a list of the words in this story.

Common words:

an	big	in
and	he	

Other words:

Alan	dark
animal	dawn
animals	dogs
bats	frogs
cats	from

Alan loves animals.

He loves bats!

Alan has ten rats ...

and ten big cats!

Alan loves animals.

He loves hogs!

Alan has ten frogs ...

and ten wild dogs!

Alan loves animals, and from dawn till dark ...

Alan works in an animal park!

Animal Park

Puzzle Time

Can you find these pictures in the story?

c

d

Which pages are the pictures from?

Turn over for answers!

Answers

The pictures come from these pages:

a. pages 4 and 5

b. pages 18 and 19

c. pages 20 and 21

d. pages 14 and 15

First published in 2010 by
Franklin Watts
338 Euston Road
London
NW1 3BH

Franklin Watts Australia
Level 17/207 Kent Street
Sydney
NSW 2000

A CIP catalogue record for this book is available from the British Library.

ISBN 978 0 7496 9384 8 (hbk)
ISBN 978 0 7496 9396 1 (pbk)

Series Editor: Jackie Hamley
Series Advisors: Dr Hilary Minns and Catherine Glavina
Series Designer: Peter Scoulding

Printed in China

Franklin Watts is a division of Hachette Children's Books, an Hachette UK company. www.hachette.co.uk